Walt Disney

Sleeping Beauty

TWIN BOOKS

B. Mitchell

Once upon a time, there was a King named Stephen, who lived in a tall palace with his beautiful Queen. They were good and kind and were loved by their subjects. Nearby, in another kingdom, lived their friend, King Hubert.

The two realms had a peaceful existence —almost perfect— except for one problem.

King Hubert had a son, Prince Philip. But alas, King Stephen and his wife had no children.

One day, to everyone's joy, the Queen gave birth to
a baby girl. She was called Aurora, which means sunrise,
because that's when she was born.

Bells rang throughout the two kingdoms. The glad
news was spread all over the land. The King and Queen
ordered a great feast. Everyone was invited to celebrate
their daughter's birth.

On the day of the feast,
crowds of people began to
arrive at the palace.

Ladies in silken gowns,
lords in furs and velvet, and
knights in bright armor,
entered through the palace
gates.

Everyone wanted to see the
Princess.

King Hubert and his son Prince Philip were the first to see the baby Princess. "Congratulations, she's a beautiful child!" King Hubert cried.

Not only was he happy for his friend, but he was also thinking about the future. The two Kings had been hoping that one day their kingdoms would be united. Now, this dream would come true. When Princess Aurora grew up, she and Prince Philip would be married. The little Prince looked down at the baby... it was hard to believe that this little thing would one day be his wife.

Suddenly, a shimmering
golden light filled the room.
Three fairies appeared
wearing pointed hats and
waving magic wands. These
were the three good fairies
who kept watch over the
kingdom: Flora, Fauna and
Merryweather.

Although they were usually invisible, the King knew that he could count on their help in times of difficulty. The King had invited them to his daughter's christening, and each fairy brought a gift. Flora was the first to speak. "Princess Aurora, I give you the gift of beauty."

She waved her wand and a shimmering cloud of golden sparks filled the room.

Next came Fauna. "I will give you the joy of music," she said. "You shall have the most beautiful voice in the realm." As she lifted her wand, a chorus of birds flew above the cradle.

13

Finally, it was Merry-
weather's turn to give her
present to the Princess. She
had a very kind heart but
was a bit forgetful. "Prince.
Oh sorry! I mean Princess,
I shall give you... Oh dear!
Now what was it that I was
going to give her?" she said,
stopping to think.

But before she could
continue a great gust of wind
burst open the windows.
A blinding light entered the
room. Everyone cried out in
horror.

A terrifying flash of lightning announced the appearance of a tall woman. Dressed in a long black cape and wearing a headdress with two black horns, she looked like the devil himself.

A gasp spread across the room. "It's Maleficent, the evil fairy!" murmured the crowd. "What's she doing here?"

"I AM HERE BECAUSE SOMEONE FORGOT TO INVITE ME!" she screamed. "Isn't that so, your Majesty?" she demanded. "But I have not forgotten to bring a gift! I too have something special for your daughter! You shall pay for your neglect, my dear King Stephen!" she said with a wicked laugh.

Pointing to the baby, Maleficent cried, "Princess Aurora, you have received many gifts. Use them well, for you will not have them for long. Before your sixteenth birthday you will prick your finger on a spindle and you will DIE!"

People gasped in horror. Cries were heard throughout the large room.

King Stephen could barely contain his anger. However, he knew that his daughter's life was in danger. He calmly spoke to Maleficent. "Madame, what you say is true. I did forget to invite you. It is I who am guilty—not the child. Look at that innocent baby. She has done you no harm. Please, take pity on her."

Silence reigned over the room. The people held their breaths, waiting for Maleficent to reply.

"It's too late, Your Majesty! This will teach you that I NEVER FORGET AND I NEVER FORGIVE!"

The King turned to his soldiers. "Seize her! Put her in chains!" he ordered. But before the soldiers could touch her, Maleficent was gone! She'd vanished in a burst of green flames! The unhappy Queen clutched the baby in her arms.

Merryweather broke the stunned silence. "Calm down everyone. I shall do what I can to help. If only I could remember what it was... Oh yes, now I know. I cannot undo the evil spell, but I shall soften it a little." The kind little fairy waved her magic wand. "Princess Aurora, if you prick your finger before your sixteenth birthday—you will not die! Instead you will fall into a deep sleep. A lover's kiss will awaken you. And then you shall live happily ever after."

King Hubert tried to comfort his friends. "Listen to me. I know how we can protect the Princess. We must burn all the spinning wheels. If there are no spinning wheels, there will be no spindles, and no needles to harm the Princess."

"Hurrah!" shouted the crowd. Messengers were sent to every town and village. Thousands of spinning wheels were collected and brought to the palace. A large bonfire was lit. Nothing remained of the spinning wheels but ashes. Princess Aurora would be safe.

However, the three good fairies were not so sure of this solution. They knew Maleficent too well. It wasn't easy to fight her. Together they decided that something more had to be done.

Aurora must be taken far away from the palace. She must be taken to a secret place.

"We'll hide her in the forest," said Fauna. "She'll be safe with us."

"I know," said Flora, "we'll dress up as peasant women. She can be our orphan niece. No one will find her."

With a wave of a wand, the fairies were transformed into peasant women. But now the most difficult part—to convince the King and Queen.

And indeed, it wasn't easy.
"But then it will be as if we
didn't have a child," said the
King.

"Yes, but just think, if
she's with us, she'll live after
she is 16. We promise to
look after her and bring her
back," replied Merryweather.

"Where will you hide her?"
asked the Queen.

"In the woodcutter's
cottage in the middle of the
forest. Maleficent will never
find her there."

And so, late one night
three little figures were seen
leaving the palace.
Watching them were the
King and Queen, sad to see
their daughter leave.

Several days later, the three women arrived at their destination. The woodcutter who had lived there had been dead for many years. The house was empty. "Not much a of place for a Princess," sighed Merryweather.

Flora scolded her. "Remember, we are here to hide her. You must never say the word Princess again. From now on we are simple peasants and she is our niece!"

"What do we call her?" asked Fauna.

It took several moments before they could decide on a name. "Briar Rose!" said Flora. "She is like a wild rose, lost in the forest." And so the three women looked after the little Princess. They gave her all the love and care of real parents.

The years passed. The blond baby had grown into a beautiful young girl, with a smile always on her lovely face. She was as pretty as a wild rose, blossoming in the middle of the forest.

Soon she would be 16. It was impossible to think that
nearly 16 years had passed since they came to live in
the forest. The thought of giving her back to her parents
made the fairies a bit sad. "We mustn't be selfish," said
Fauna. "Think of her parents. We've had her all these
years. They shall be overjoyed to see their daughter
again."

Someone else was counting
the days, months and years
that passed. Maleficent, too,
was watching the time go by.
She had searched high and
low for the Princess.

Her soldiers always
returned with the same reply.
"No Princess."

On this day, sparks flew from her eyes, the horns of her headdress began to shake. "You imbeciles! Worthless creatures! I'll have to find her myself! Beware, Aurora, I shall find you!" screamed the evil Maleficent.

Maleficent went to see her
faithful friend – the raven.
"You, Raven, are not like
the others. Use your sharp
eyes and wits! I'm sure that
you can find her," she said,
caressing his feathers.
"Fly away! Find the Princess!"

The Raven flew high into the sky until it was no more than a tiny speck. It dived and swept over every town and village.

If anyone could find Princess Aurora, it would be the Raven.

At the cottage, the three fairies were making plans for Briar Rose's birthday. They wanted to surprise her and so they sent her out into the forest to pick wild berries.

Fauna was going to bake a birthday cake. She looked up a recipe in her big book. There were so many kinds of cakes. "Ah! Here's one that sounds delicious!" she said, and began mixing and stirring.

Flora and Merryweather were going to make a dress. "You stand still and I'll try this cloth on you," said Flora, as she began winding cloth around poor Merryweather.

While the three fairies were busy at the cottage, Briar
Rose wandered through the forest, picking wild berries.
Her friends, the owl, bluebirds, robins and the squirrel
joined her. When her basket was full, Briar Rose
stopped and sang a song that her aunts had taught her.

Briar Rose did not know that the sound of her singing had carried through the woods. A young horseman stopped when he heard her sweet voice. "Who is singing that pretty song?" wondered the young man. "She can't be far from here."

Briar Rose had begun to daydream and dance while she sang her love song. She did not hear the young man come up behind her.

"Shall we dance?" he asked holding her arms.

Briar Rose turned. "Who are you?" she asked. This was the man of her dreams.

"Your friend, if you'll let me," said the young man.

While the two young people danced, the Owl said to his companions, "Do you know who that is? That's Prince Philip, King Hubert's son."

"Oh! I bet he doesn't know that he's dancing with a real princess," said the squirrel.

"Shush!" said the Owl. "No one is supposed to say that word!"

It was getting late.
Briar Rose remembered the
wild berries and her waiting
aunts.

"I must go now," she said,
and started to run away.

"Wait!" called the Prince.
"I don't even know your
name or where you live."

But Briar Rose had been
told by her aunts never to
speak to strangers. She didn't
want to disobey them any
more than she had already.

Back at the cottage, the three aunts were in a panic. "Get me out of here!" cried Merryweather, who was all tied up in the dress.

"I can't help you!" cried Fauna. "Look! The cake is starting to fall!"

The three aunts were desperate. Briar Rose would return any minute and everything was a mess!

Flora rubbed her chin. "I know. We'll use our magic wands. After all, this is a special occasion."

"Why of course! I'd almost forgotten we still had them," said Fauna.

Three waves of the magic wand and a beautiful gown was made!

"I was never much of a cook anyway," said Fauna, as she let her wand do the work.

"Now that's what I call a magic recipe," she said as a scrumptious-looking cake appeared.

There was just one slight problem – the color of the dress. Merryweather thought that blue was best. "It will match her eyes!" she said as she waved her wand.

"NO! NO! NO! Red is
better. It will go with her
rosy cheeks," said Flora.

"I said blue!" cried
Merryweather as she shot off
sparks from her wand.

The fairies began sending flashes of color all over the house. They had forgotten that they were supposed to be careful and not use their magic.

Sparks of color flew out the chimney. The evil Raven was flying by and spotted the cottage.

He swooped down to have a closer look.

"Caw! Caw! Magic! Magic!" he croaked. "I must go and tell Maleficent," he said, as he flew off to inform the wicked fairy.

Hearing Briar Rose's footsteps outside, the fairies stopped fighting.

"Surprise!" they shouted as she entered the room. Briar Rose was delighted. What a beautiful gown, and the cake looked delicious!

"We decided to celebrate your birthday one day early," said Flora. "Tomorrow is a very special day. You will go to meet your parents—the King and Queen."

"Yes, you are not really Briar Rose," said Fauna. "Your real name is Princess Aurora and your parents live in a palace far away from here."

"I too have something to tell you," said Aurora, and she told them about the young man in the forest.

Early the next morning the fairies and the Princess set out for the palace. Princess Aurora hid beneath a long cloak. As she walked, she thought of the young man whom she'd met in the forest.

The fairies thought of that day 16 years ago, when they had crept through the woods with a little baby in their arms.

At the palace the two kings were beginning to celebrate when the Prince told his father that he could not marry Princess Aurora. His heart was lost to the young girl in the forest.

Aurora had secretly entered the palace. She was to wait for her parents to come and find her. While she waited, she explored her room. She saw a little door.

Curious, she opened it and stepped into another room. There was someone inside... a tall woman dressed in black. "Come here my lovely Princess," said the strange woman. "I have a gift for you. Look at this beautiful spinning wheel. Go ahead! Touch it – it's yours!"

Aurora put out her hand to touch the beautiful wood and her finger was pricked by the needle.

All at once she fell to the floor.

"I have my revenge!" cried Maleficent as she stared down at the fallen Princess. "Now all I have to do is capture the Prince. He musn't find her and give her the kiss that will save her." Maleficent disappeared in a puff of smoke.

It was the three good fairies who found Aurora. "We must do something quickly!" said Flora. "We can't let her poor parents find her like this."

"Yes, and we must find the Prince before Maleficent does," said Fauna.

"But Aurora told us that she was in love with the man in the forest. What are we going to do?" asked Flora. "Remember, only her lover's kiss can save her."

The three fairies put their heads together. At last they decided to put everyone in the palace to sleep. Waving their wands, the three fairies flew around the palace. Soon, everyone was fast asleep.

"What next?" asked Flora.

"If Aurora loves the man in the forest, we'll have to find him—whoever he is," said Fauna.

And so Flora, Fauna and Merryweather went off to search in the forest. Soon they met the Owl. After they had told him what had happened, the wise Owl said, "I know who the young man is that Aurora loves. It is in fact Prince Philip. And he's on his way to the wood-cutter's cottage to look for her."

Indeed, the Prince was hunting. He had told his father
that he would not marry the Princess. He was in love
with a peasant girl who lived in the forest.

"This must be her house," he said when he saw the
cottage. He could hear someone moving inside. He
knocked on the door.

The door swung open and the Prince stepped into the room. Before he knew what was happening, a dozen creatures jumped on him.

The Prince was powerless. They were too fast. Soon he was tied up and couldn't move. The creatures led him into another room.

A tall woman dressed in black was waiting for him. "The one you're looking for is not here," she said in a dry voice. "You'll never find her. You are my prisoner and you'll never escape from where I'm going to put you. Take him away!" commanded Maleficent, who then vanished in a flash of light.

Seeing smoke coming from their cottage, the fairies rushed to the scene. "Someone's been here!" cried Flora.

"I smell smoke—Maleficent was here. And look! Here is the Prince's cap!" cried Merryweather.

There was no time to waste. There was only one place to look for the Prince—the castle of Shadows!

Philip was chained to the walls of the deepest darkest dungeon in the castle. No one would be able to find him. "Why are you keeping me here?" he demanded of Maleficent.

The evil woman smiled and said, "I've known you for many years. Don't you remember, 16 years ago..."

When she had finished telling him of her spell, she added, "Your little peasant girl is Princess Aurora. You shall never marry her now!" Then she left the dungeon.

The Prince strained at the chains—but they were too strong. "I must escape from here," he said.

At that moment, three little shapes flew in through the bars. It was the three fairies.

"We are Briar Rose's godmothers," said Flora.

"No, not Briar Rose, Aurora," said Fauna.

"Look, this is no time to argue," said Flora, who waved her wand and broke the chains holding the Prince.

"Here, take this Shield of Truth," instructed Flora. With a flash a shield appeared. "And, this Sword of Valor!" she commanded, as a sword flew into his hand.

"Go to the palace. The Princess is there waiting for your kiss."

The Prince, armed with his shield and sword, rushed off to find his Princess. However, Maleficent saw him leave. "He has escaped me, but not for long," she screamed. "I shall wait for him at the palace."

Nearing the palace, the Prince found himself surrounded by an enormous hedge of thorns.

"This is Maleficent's work," he thought, as he swung his sword and hacked at the thorns.

After fighting his way through the nasty thorns, the Prince reached the bridge to the palace.

A heavy silence surrounded him. Just then an enormous gust of wind blew toward him. It was a burning wind, violent and evil-smelling.

Suddenly a large dark shadow appeared through the mist. It was an enormous black dragon!

"Maleficent!" cried Philip, recognizing his enemy. A wicked laugh sounding like thunder came from the dragon.

The dragon opened its enormous mouth and out roared flames and poison gas. Quickly Philip held up his magic shield. The flames could not touch him.

The horrible monster came
closer. It smashed everything
in its path and spat flames as
it advanced toward the
Prince.

Philip took up his Sword
of Valor. He swung back his
arm and threw the sword
with all his might. The steel
flew straight into the
dragon's heart.

A mighty crash was heard
as it fell dead.

Now that the path was free, the Prince rushed past the sleeping guards, guests and servants, into the palace. There in a bedroom lay the beautiful young girl from the forest.

"So this is Princess Aurora," said the Prince softly as he looked at her. He bent down and gave her a kiss. Aurora opened her eyes. "You're the man from the forest," she said.

"And you are Princess Aurora," replied the Prince smiling.

Meanwhile the fairies were busy awakening everyone. No one was aware that any time had passed. The two Kings continued their conversation as if nothing had occurred.

"I'm sure that the two young people will like each other," said King Hubert.

"Yes, of course," King Stephen agreed. "It's time for Aurora to arrive."

"Mother! Father!" a sweet voice called out.

There before them stood their daughter.

"Aurora! My lovely child!" cried the Queen. Look at you! You're a beautiful young girl!" She ran to hug her daughter. What joy it was for these three, parents and child, to be reunited after so long.

Philip introduced Aurora to his father.

"We've already met," laughed the jolly King. "Although, she was only a tiny bit of a thing!"

Then, blushing with pleasure, Philip and Aurora announced their plans. They wanted to marry.

The two Kings were overjoyed. Their wishes would now come true.

A great and joyful ball was given in honor of the Prince and Princess. But whenever the dancing music stopped, three little voices could be heard chattering away. They were the voices of Flora, Fauna and Merryweather, for although the fairies had become invisible, nothing could keep them from watching over their precious Princess.

This edition published by W.H. Smith Publishers, Canada.

Produced by
Twin Books
15 Sherwood Place
Greenwich, CT. 06830.

ISBN 0 86124 319 6

Printed and bound in Spain

Reprinted 1987